FOLLOW THE ZOOKEEPER

By Patricia Relf • Illustrated by Carolyn Bracken

With thanks to the Buffalo Zoological Gardens, Buffalo, N.Y., and African Lion Safari, Rockton, Ontario

A GOLDEN BOOK • NEW YORK
Western Publishing Company, Inc. Racine, Wisconsin 53404

ISBN 0-307-11888-6/ISBN 0-307-61888-9 (lib. bdg.)   F G H I J

It was early morning at the zoo. The head zookeeper, Mr. Scott, was just coming to work. Ducks and geese waddled toward him, quacking and honking. As soon as they saw Mr. Scott, they knew it was almost time for breakfast.

Mr. Scott stopped to check the message board. One note was good news. Two alligator eggs had hatched during the night. Another note said the gorilla keeper was sick and wouldn't be coming in to work.

"I'd better make breakfast for the gorillas if Joe is out sick today," said Mr. Scott to himself.

In the kitchen, the keeper who looked after the lions and tigers was slicing big pieces of meat. The bear keeper had filled one bucket with fish. Now he was pouring dry food into a second bucket.

PRIMATE BISCUITS

RODENT FOOD

DOG MEAT (for Bears)

OT ITS

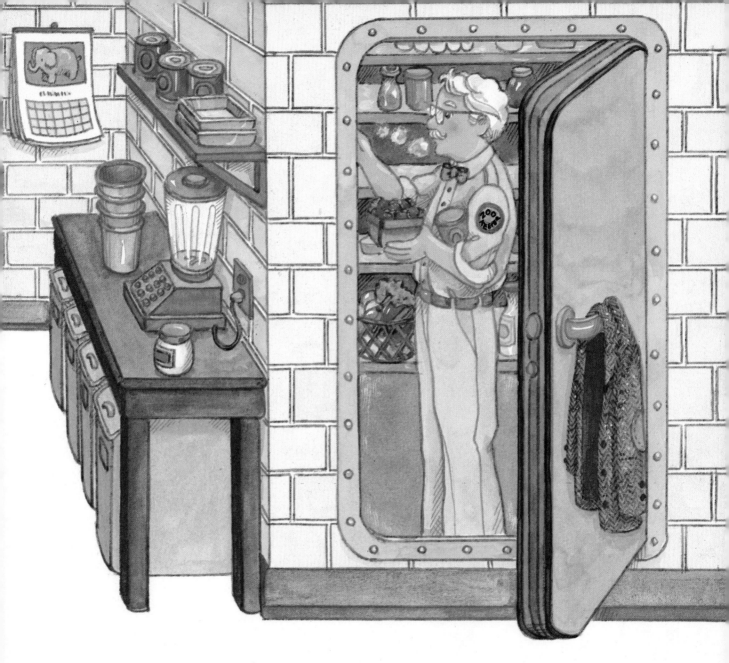

Mr. Scott found some yogurt and a box of ripe
strawberries. He mixed them with vitamin powder
in a blender to make milkshakes for the gorillas.

Mr. Scott went to the building where the gorillas lived. When he turned on the lights, Bo and Carol jumped up and rattled the bars on their cages. Then they reached out eagerly for their breakfast.

Bo and Carol drank the milkshakes. They didn't spill a drop. When they were all through, Mr. Scott pulled a lever. "Time to go outside," he said.

The back door of each gorilla cage opened. Bo and Carol ran out into their daytime play area. Now Mr. Scott could clean the gorillas' indoor cages.

Next Mr. Scott went to the zoo
pond to see the two new baby
alligators.

But by the time he got there, there were three new babies! They made croaking noises as they walked around the nest.

Mr. Scott's next stop was the Animals of the Night building. In the building bright lights had burned all night. Now Mr. Scott turned them off.

The animals began to wake up. They thought that night had come. They were ready to eat and play.

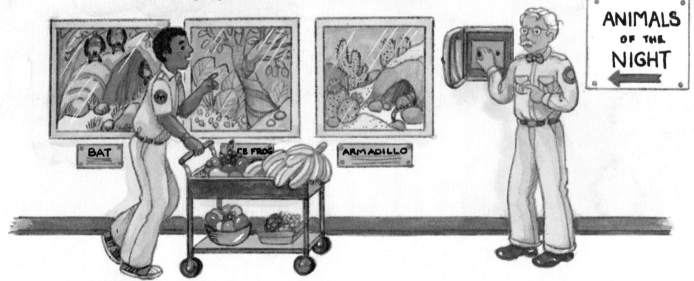

Mr. Scott turned on a red light so that visitors would be able to see the animals. The nighttime animals didn't seem to notice the light.

When Mr. Scott went outside, he saw people at the main gate waiting for the zoo to open. The cafeteria and the souvenir shop were ready for visitors. The hot dog and balloon sellers were waiting for business to begin. One of the guards unlocked the gate. The zoo was open for the day.

Mr. Scott climbed into a jeep and started a tour of the big, open sections of the zoo. First he drove to the African Safari Park to see the lions. A big male lion was still gnawing on a breakfast bone. A female lion was sleeping. Young cubs were tussling on the rocks nearby.

Mr. Scott drove on to see the zebras. They came close to him when he offered them apples. While they ate, Mr. Scott looked carefully at their hooves. A zebra's hoof grows all the time, like a fingernail. Sometimes it needs to be trimmed. But the rocks inside the zebras' enclosure were wearing down the zebras' hooves, so they didn't need trimming.

Mr. Scott climbed back in his jeep and drove on.

He drove past the antelopes and ostriches. Mr. Scott played his usual game with the ostriches. He held a small piece of meat out the window of the jeep. The ostriches ran after the tasty treat. A large female ostrich was the first to catch up. She grabbed the prize from Mr. Scott.

It was time for lunch. Mr. Scott parked in a shady spot and unwrapped his sandwiches. Suddenly he felt someone nudge his shoulder. A curious baby giraffe wanted to share Mr. Scott's lunch.

"Sorry, little fellow," said Mr. Scott. "Eat your nice hay. This food is for me!"

After lunch, Mr. Scott drove into the North American Animals section. Debbie, one of Mr. Scott's helpers, was fixing a broken fence rail.

"Fred and Marcus, two of the elk, had a fight this morning and knocked the fence down," Debbie said. "Fred scraped a leg, so I sent him to the hospital."

Mr. Scott told Debbie he would visit Fred the elk.

Mr. Scott drove back to the central part of the zoo. At the animal hospital he saw Fred the elk. Dr. Rose, the veterinarian, said Fred's leg wound was nothing to worry about.

Mr. Scott went inside to see Sandy, a tiny tiger cub whose mother had died. Dr. Rose fed Sandy five times a day with a baby bottle. While Mr. Scott was playing with Sandy, Dr. Rose got a call.

Mr. Scott went with Dr. Rose to examine the rhino, who seemed tired. Dr. Rose didn't think he was really sick, but she took a blood sample so she could do some tests. She asked the keeper about the rhino's diet and suggested extra vitamins.

Next Mr. Scott visited his old friends the elephants. He had once been the elephant keeper, and the animals still remembered him.

As soon as Mr. Scott appeared, an elephant named Big Bill stuck out his tongue. He loved to have Mr. Scott rub his tongue. Clara, the baby elephant, found some peanuts in Mr. Scott's pockets.

That afternoon Mr. Scott talked to some school children about baby animals born at the zoo.

Later he went to his office in the administration building. He wrote out a report for the director of the zoo and checked the bills for the animals' food.

Then Mr. Scott went to the reptile house to receive a very special package. It was a Burmese python, which had been sent from a zoo across the country. The giant snake looked healthy and began to slither around its new home.

As Mr. Scott walked back to his office, he saw a worker cleaning up the litter on the paths. The zoo was closed for the day.

Mr. Scott's busy day was over. It was time for him to go home.

"Good night, everybody," he said to the ducks and the geese. But they didn't hear him. They were already asleep.

STAFF
EXIT